NELLIE K.

UNREGISTERED
Stories

UNREGISTERED

Cover design, illustrations and back cover photograph by Umit Kartoglu
Typset and interior design: Maraton Dizgievi • www.dizgievi.com
Printed by CreateSpace, An Amazon.com Company

First published March 2016
http://nelliek.ch/unregistered
unregistered@nelliek.ch

ISBN softcover 978-2-9701065-2-4
ISBN eBook 978-2-9701065-3-1

Nellie K.

UN(Я)EGISTERED

Stories

to my family...

CONTENTS

LALA,
MY REDHEAD,
MY RUBY

St. Todor's Day, or Horse Easter, has been honored by the Kalaidzhi Roma throughout generations. Celebrating the start of spring and the health of the horse, young Gypsy men used to compete in riding. On this day of the biggest horse fair, families also traded their daughters into marriages.

Mis ojos
*que exploraron la tristeza**
Pablo Neruda

On its way over the faraway hills, the sun suffused the valley with blazing gold as if reaffirming its undeniable power over every living thing. Blinded by the sun, the horse reared and halted the carriage. Velcho loosened the reins to let the horse gather its senses. A gentle breeze set in, subsuming Velcho into its invigorating freshness. Retreating, the sun softened. The clouds swirled, slowly brushing the sky in pink, yellow and purple. The valley that had cradled Velcho as a child welcomed him back with a mesmerizing sunset.

---

* *My eyes that explored sadness.*

He thought of Lela. It was in this valley that their caravans had always made their final stop before returning home in the fall. In the fading sunlight far out by the forest line, still lived the memory of the two of them laughing and frolicking in piles of crisp foliage.

Watching them play, Lela's mother thought that they would make a beautiful couple one day. Thinking and dreaming was the guilty pleasure she was reprimanded for by her husband alongside their tribe's disapproval of her reading skills. Back then she was one of the very few Gypsy women who could read. Succumbing to the common opinion, her husband asked her to keep it to herself.

At night, once the men had fallen asleep, exhausted from work and travel, Lela's mother read the stories of *The Arabian Nights* to her little girl. Colorful by day, the wagon's tapestry would lose its gypsy glitter under the starry sky. Livened by the flickering candlelight, the wagon stood out mysteriously in the darkness, calling for the little boy to steal up on it. He was enchanted by the music of the woman's voice and by her power of word. His occasional fidgeting let her know that he was there, but she pretended she heard nothing and read louder instead. Sinbad's bravery and Ali Baba's wisdom fascinated Velcho.

The book held a special meaning for Lela's mother. During one of their travels through a city, she took her little daughter to a bookshop. No Gypsy was allowed in. They looked at the window display, respectfully keeping their distance. Lela's mother read the book titles outloud. Amazed by the colorful covers, Lela joyfully jumped and clapped her hands. An old man came out, heading toward them. Used to being chased away, they hurried to leave. The man followed. Breathing heavily, he caught up with them and handed a book to Lela, saying that it was his gift to her mother, a Gypsy lady, who had surprised him that she could read. The man bowed respectfully and walked away. Lela's mother burst into tears, and when she calmed down, the two of them slowly walked back to the camp in silence. The book stayed hidden under a pile of clothes. On the nights of long journeys, it brought to life stories of incredible adventures.

Velcho could no longer remember the name of Lela's mother who died giving birth to Lela's sister. Lela had kept the old book of *The Arabian Nights*. It smelled of her mother and something that she learned later all books smelled of – the magic of knowledge.

Velcho looked around. The patches of melting snow, glistening in the fading sun, reminded him of the treasures of *The Forty Thieves*. He felt as if the valley spoke to him with the beautiful memories that they both shared. He felt free and pure.

The sky dimmed into twilight, blurring the horizon. Velcho's heart pounded at the thought of the morning when Vano would place his beautiful daughter, Lela, on a bridal display at St Todor's Day market.

Velcho worked hard, making and selling tinware, and repairing roofs all over Bulgaria and as far as Austria. He was well prepared to bid for his Lela. He reined in the horse with a loud whistle. The horse jerked forward impatiently, rattling the jugs and pots he had not sold.

* * *

A man worked his way through the heavily perfumed crowd at the Gypsy bride market of Kalaidzhi. Fast and steady with confidence, he kept pulling his seventeen-year-old daughter behind him. His sun-and-wind-withered face wore no emotion; only his light grey eyes betrayed an uncertainty that no one noticed. He looked at no one.

That day St Todor's market boasted the most beautiful girls on display to adorn the families of the richest grooms. Everything was arranged to the best of tradition. The brightest of colors, the finest of clothes had long been prepared for the occasion. Ceremonial bread baked in the shape of a horseshoe was offered around. Warm Rakia soothed the capriciousness of the rich and brightened the gloominess of the poor. The air was charged with the euphoria of bargain. The DJ blasted garish pop until the time came to dance the traditional Horo to the singing accompaniment of older women.

* * *

Dana tightened her grip on her father's hand. With a stern face, he pushed his way toward the center of the field where negotiations on the brides' prices and dowries had already begun. Young girls willingly displayed their best to the evaluating eyes of men and their families. They looked all alike with their identity lost under globs of mascara and layers of powder and rouge.

Dana felt as though in a sales outlet surrounded by mannequins in flashy mini-dresses, towering above her on heels. She could not stop thinking how humiliating it was to be an object for sale.

* * *

Two years earlier Dana's best friend, Donka, was sold to an older man. Her family vehemently obliged with the Kalaidzhi tradition of not mixing their daughter with boys, and, although a brilliant student, she had to leave school before she turned fourteen.

Donka stayed at home for a year, learning to take care of the household, and watching her mother, Lana, tend to her father's needs. Donka sank into depression next to Lana, who lived her life with a heavy sense of guilt. Lana could not have more children, for which she was judged severely by her husband's family. In her loveless marriage, Donka was her only joy. But consumed with sadness and guilt, Lana did not know how to show her love to her only child. She felt awkward and tense around her.

Zealous of the traditions, Donka's father had carefully calculated whom to sell her to as a bride.

Newlywed Donka was no longer allowed to see Dana who remained at school against the tradition. Sad and lonely, Donka died in delivery.

The thought of Donka's death persecuted Dana. According to an old Roma tradition, which considers delivery impure, Donka was put in a barn away from the family. The old woman put there to assist her fell asleep. Donka did not call for help. She chose to bleed away silently.

Lana died soon after, followed by her husband. Their departure was considered impure.

* * *

"Who knows what story is behind each of these made-up faces," Dana thought.

She came here with a heavy feeling. Her father thought of the bride market tradition as shameful and futile, but he had sunk deeper and deeper into debt. With cheap pots and pans from China, no one wanted to buy from traditional tinsmiths anymore. The little money that Petko made repairing roofs was barely enough to make ends meet. Although Dana deeply disapproved of the tradition, she had taken weeks to convince Petko to arrange her marriage.

"I want you to find me a good husband, tatko,* I truly do!"

She carefully avoided mentioning their financial hardship.

Defying Kalaidhzi traditions, Petko encouraged Dana to con-

———————————

* *father*

tinue her studies in Stara Zagora after she had finished school. He wanted Dana to be like other Bulgarian women, educated and free. For her happiness, he would shed traditions and become an outcast. But Dana came back asking for a husband. Little did he know that her true intention was to save him from his debt.

* * *

The news of Petko's decision to announce Dana as a bride spread fast. She was expected to hit the highest price in years, just like her mother did when Petko's father bought her against a rival family. Back then Petko's family had wealth and power. Despite his recent impoverishment, his appearance at the market caused a stir of jealousy and admiration.

"*Petko?!*"

A woman hurled herself at him from across the crowd. Maria had not seen her brother-in-law since her sister had passed away. She let a few tears leave a thin trace through her rouge-and-powder mask and stamped a loud smack on Dana's cheek.

"*You look just like Lela! Come with me to meet my girls!*"

Knowing how much Petko disliked his sister-in-law, Dana hesitated.

"*Keep walking,*" he said, pulling her away.

"*Wait! She cannot be shown around looking like this,*" Maria shouted above the crowd. "*She needs makeup! And a hairdresser!*"

Confused by this emotional encounter, Dana kept looking back. The crowd closed behind them, blocking Maria who pushed persistently after them. Knowing little of her mother's family, Dana longed to learn more. She had heard that her grandfather took to drinking after his wife died, leaving him with their newborn baby, Maria, and her mother, Lela. Lela raised her sister and took care of their father. She was sold to Petko's family against her will, but it did not take her long to fall deeply in love with Petko.

In the midst of the festive crowd Maria's chiming lost its volume. Breathless, Maria gave up her pursuit. The unbearable heaviness of frustration pulled her down to her knees, and there she sat amid the raucous laughing crowd and wailed over her own marriage full of misery, violence and deception.

The music boomed, deafening the crowd and intoxicating the young who went giddy at this rare opportunity to mix, hold hands and build hopes ever so elusive.

Maria raised her head to the spotless blue sky. As a child, she believed that this was a sign of good to come her way. But years passed by, and she had shut down all illusionary hopes. Instead, she had somehow nurtured herself into a calculative, cunning woman, whose morale had long lost its value. Her fox-like deceitful nature was what Petko despised her for.

* * *

"Kalaidzhi do not marry outside the tribe. Our family is the oldest... the best of the Kalaidzhi... There's only one man I see as worthy of you...from a once rival family... but time's changed. They offered a lot of money for you last year. I refused... They say that their son, Roman, is smart and kind. He is a student in Brussels. It's rare for us, Gypsies. I'll agree only if you like him, and if he promises to help you study too. I want you to meet all other grooms tomorrow, and then we'll see. I want a different life for you, Dana. Your mother's will was that you be educated and free to choose your life. By taking you to the market, I go against her will."

"She'd have approved, tatko. I know she would!"

* * *

The house was empty and cold. Velcho lit the stove and brought in the blankets from his caravan. Plasters of paint fell off the once-white walls of the rooms, baring muddy patches. The stone floor lost its old shine under a thick layer of dust. Except for Velcho, no one came here anymore. His father died in jail, falsely accused of robbery. Years of waiting withered his mother out. The villagers turned their backs on them, and by the time their name was cleared, sadness, shame, and loneliness had taken his mother far away. Velcho, the youngest of five sons, was the only one to remain in the village. He refused to flee the shame that was not just. Later on, he realized that it was rather his love for Lela that had kept him there.

Lela's deep green eyes harbored his free soul, her voice lulled him into the serenity a Gypsy might search for but never find, her silky skin felt as liberating as the first warm breeze in early spring, her golden hair was the sun that never set, calling for new horizons.

"Lela, my valley, my journey, my home," he thought, falling asleep.

* * *

Petko lost Lela to uterus cancer when Dana was seven. He did not remarry or fall in love again and raised Dana all by himself. Coming from one of the oldest and most respected Kalaidzhi families, although no longer rich, Petko was now pressured by both his clan and his daughter to choose her a husband. He himself met his beautiful Lela at the bride market. Now, back to the market, he felt as if he was back to that same day in March when he first saw her. Cold sweat streamed down his temples. There she stood that rainy day. The aloofness and the unbending pride of her very straight posture immediately set her apart from the crowd taken with the anxiety of bargain. Her unusually green eyes kept shooting fiery arrows of contempt in disapproval of being sold alongside horses.

Now, Petko was expected to trade his own daughter's life. He loathed himself for bringing Dana here.

* * *

Dana took the beautiful looks of her mother, yet in such a different way. Her skin was not so fair, its olive hue created a striking harmony with her green eyes, adorned by a dark layer of velvet lashes. She did not have the proud regal look of her mother. Instead, her eyes radiated the soft wisdom of a mature child. The blush in her cheeks seemed to be a reflection of her red curls gently streaming down her face.

According to a Roma tradition, Dana also had a secret name of which neither her, nor her father, nor others were to know. Her mother had given it to her at birth in order to confuse the evil spirits and turn them away from her baby, who was born with long red hair.

"Lala, my redhead, my ruby," her mother called her in her prayers.

Just like her mother, Dana carried herself very straight. She was not as tall, though, and her soft and gentle nature brought out a confusing touch of shy fragility to her entire look.

Just like Lela, Dana deeply disapproved of the tradition to be sold into a marriage. But she came here willingly with a purpose her father would never know.

* * *

Velcho prepared to offer the highest bid for his Lela.

He was up before dawn, weakened by a sleepless night and an unusual anxiety. He washed with ice-cold water and put on a fresh white shirt that his mother embroidered. He looked around the empty room, once full of life and joy. He thought of his mother laughing, his father playing guitar, their friends and family singing at the festive table. Now, his caravan was his home. His horse was his only companion on the long exhausting journeys in the search for work and the meaning of life he could not see without Lela.

* * *

The morning was dull, the weather did not promise much sun to celebrate the start of spring. A canvas was pulled over a circle of wagons, harboring the display stage for brides. Young girls were brought in and patiently waited for the horse race and trades to complete.

Velcho was met with a loud cheer when he galloped into the fair's field - the clan was happy to see an offspring from the oldest family. Mitko, an arrogant competitor from a rival family, measured Velcho with a self-complacent look, reining in his horse at the start line.

Velcho's mustang darted like an arrow, leaving everyone in the dust. On his horse Velcho was no longer a human. He was a flying free spirit. He was the wind, the sun, and the hills. He was one with nature. He bolted through the finish line to the loud cheering of the crowd. He needed no horse, neither to buy nor to sell. Having won the race, he headed straight to the brides' stage.

Young girls in their finest dresses promptly exhibited their pushed up bosoms. Older women were seated all around, throwing judgmental looks to their daughters' rivals and grooms-to-be. Heavy rain broke in, forcing the canvas to leak and the girls to cling together.

Velcho's arrival stirred the female crowd with excitement. Anyone would have wanted to be his wife.

He saw Lela getting off the stage, helped by a man. Holding an umbrella, the man accompanied Lela to a small richly dressed crowd. Her father was there too. She was asked to open her mouth, and they all looked at her teeth with a nod of approval. She was then ordered to turn around and lift her long skirt to show that her feet were of small size. With her head down, face burning red, she obeyed. Asked by the men to ensure that her legs were good, an old woman bent to look under Lela's skirt. Velcho walked up when a man pinched her cheek, approving of its firmness.

"I want to bid," he said, turning to her father, Vano.

"You cannot afford her," Vano said coldly with a dismissive look.

"I want to bid," Velcho insisted. He did not look at Lela who shook with shame and anger.

Mitko came up right that moment, shouting from afar, *"She is mine, Velcho! The deal has been done while we raced. This is the business to settle between families. You have none!"*

"You have no house to take your wife to," Vano stepped in. *"You are not worthy of my daughter."*

Velcho felt his blood pounding loudly at his temples, deafening him. He clenched his fists but turned and walked away instead.

"You have no family!" echoed in his head.

Velcho took off that night to never return. He would not know that Mitko left brideless too.

Petko's father, the richest of the clan, coldly observed the scene of humiliating assessment of Lela's physique by Mitko's family. He was about to leave when he saw his son, who stubbornly refused to compete for any bride, look at Lela with admiration. He had never seen him look at anyone that way before. He headed straight to the crowd of bargainers and curious spectators that gathered around Lela. The crowd went silent.

Without wasting a word on greetings, he whispered his offer to Vano's ear. The crowd did not move, waiting for the price to be announced. But all they could get for many years of gossiping to follow was Petko's father leading Lela away.

Although in a deep despair over losing her Velcho, Lela soon realized that she could have never loved Velcho more than a dear childhood friend. She was in love and happy in her marriage.

* * *

Dana surveyed the crowd from where Petko brought her. The colorful mass of bodies swayed like waves of plastic rubbish tossing about on the shore of Varna where she once went with her father. Petko repaired roofs there when the holiday season was off.

She could not cope with the feeling of aversion that overtook her suddenly, making her want to run as far away as she could. Petko took her hand at that very moment. His warm rough palm reminded her of her obligations.

"Dana, this is Roman," Petko mumbled almost voicelessly, pointing at a handsome young man who had boisterously approached them.

Roman's eyes said, *"You are hot, baby!"*

She shivered in embarrassment but thought that she should be pleased that the man was indeed handsome. Perhaps they would fall in love with each other just like her mother and father once had.

Many suitors gathered around with their high offers. Assuming that Roman's family had offered good money to her father, Dana agreed with her father's choice. She would never know that her father had neither asked for nor accepted money. He had given her away against the honorable assurances of Roman's family to take good care of her.

* * *

Dana flew on a plane for the first time. Her husband was by her side, flirting with a stewardess.

A man in jeans and a black leather jacket, with hair tightly gelled into a ponytail, met them upon arrival. Roman spoke French to him and did not bother to introduce Dana. The man took them on a long drive.

The smell of rotting trash met them at a dark entrance. Roman led the way up the staircase. Dana followed. The man kept too close to her, touching her from behind every now and then as if by accident. Petrified, Dana clung to Roman who spoke angrily on the phone, but, annoyed, he pushed her away. They finally reached a door. A woman let them in, puffing out cigarette smoke to Dana's face. Pressing her deeply cut cleavage over Roman's chest, the woman hissed something in French, slapped his face and stomped away.

The man in the leather jacket pushed Dana into a room and locked the door. He grabbed her by the waist and slashed open the zipper of her jeans. Her dry throat forced out a hoarse cry. The man twisted her arms, angrily sputtering French, and threw her on the bed, tying her hands to the metal bedhead. He tore off her T-shirt and started biting her all over. She squirmed with pain, wailing for help. The man undressed and stuffed her mouth with his underpants. She saw a syringe in his hand. Her vision blurred at the painful piercing of the needle.

* * *

Petko could not sleep the night Dana left. The wedding went through hastily, with no memories to keep. The young couple had to leave immediately for Brussels to pursue their studies. Petko borrowed more money to ensure that in addition to the dowry long prepared by Lela, his daughter was off to a good start in her marriage.

It did not take Dana long to realize that she would never love Roman and that she was just a trophy won by Roman's boastful family, but she had kept her feelings from her father.

Roman's father, Dimitry, was content with the best bride acquisition at no expense, although his wife had spread the rumor that they had paid an insane amount of money for Dana.

"Remember, Petko," Dimirty started with a certain sense of self-satisfaction, *"my brother did not get your Lela. But we've got her daughter!"*

Dimitry burst out laughing, *"If only Mitko could see that!"*

His eyes became watery all of a sudden. *"If not for you, Mitko would be alive,"* he hissed.

Petko did not respond. Dana's wellbeing was of more concern to him. But deep in his heart, he also felt sorry for Mitko who died competing for another bride a year later, after Lela was given away to Petko.

Dark thoughts tormented Petko, sleepless and desolate, night after night. When sleep finally splintered his worries, Lela came in his dream. She stared at him with eyes full of sorrow until he woke up drenched in cold sweat.

* * *

Dimitry was having breakfast when Petko rang the bell. He told his wife to keep Petko outside until he had finished eating.

"We must not let this man disturb us at such an early hour!"

Petko waited by the gate. His heart felt heavy. Lightning shot thunderously through the rain-laden clouds.

The gate finally opened. Petko darted to the porch where Dimitry stood, sheltered from the rain, and patted his belly.

"I do not have money to lend you if that is what you are here for," he started promptly.

Petko said he only wanted news from Dana. Rain kept mercilessly pouring over him.

"What news? They just left! Calls cost money! You want to see Roman deep in debt like you are?!"

Dreadful apprehension did not allow Petko to succumb to the insult. He thanked Dimitry calmly and left. He came the next morning and the morning after, and every other morning to follow, and asked the same question. He worked hard during the day and slept poorly at night, waking up to the same dream. Lela was there all the time, whispering something he could not understand.

* * *

Helpless and desolate, Petko sat over his meager dinner of stale bread and water. He was so deeply immersed in his heavy thoughts that it took him awhile to realize that someone was banging persistently on the door.

It was Maria. He wanted to shut the door, but she swiftly plunged in.

"Please, Petko! We must talk!"

There was something in Maria's voice that made Petko let her in.

"Vitko, the boy you refused to bid for Dana, is now engaged with Lidia, my youngest. God bless you for having refused him! They are like two lovebirds! He'll get his degree in engineering soon! They'll move to the city after the wedding. I am so grateful you let us have a good groom," she kept chanting without pausing for breath.

"Maria," Petko interrupted her, *"accept my congratulations. Please leave."*

The smile went off her face, she moved closer to him and said in a low voice as if afraid that someone else would hear:

"Vitko told me that he saw Roman in Sliven last week. He went there to visit a factory for his studies and saw Roman getting out of a

bar with several blonde girls. Dana was not with him. Vitko followed them, unnoticed. They went to a hotel. Vitko waited outside and then he saw them leaving in a car with another man."

Petko's heart grew cold, his mouth felt dry and salty, his trembling fingers involuntarily tapped on the table.

"Here, drink some water. Listen, Petko, nothing is for sure, and I wish my fears were wrong, but Vitko told me that he had read in a newspaper how police busted Sliven's clubs where young girls are recruited for prostitution in Brussels. Sliven is a route for women's trafficking! This is what Vitko says! Vitko also says that Roman has never ever been a student! I am worried about Dana. I see you passing by every morning on the way to Dimitry's. Oh, that bastard! Why did you give Dana away to that family?! Petko, time has changed, you've been disconnected with all of us after Lela died. God bless her soul! You must not cut yourself from your own roots!"

Maria took Petko's trembling hands into hers.

"I say, Petko, you must go and see for yourself. Here, I brought some money. Don't bother to think of giving it back. I saved it for a rainy day, but your days are not bright, so have it all please."

A hot burning lump rolled up to his throat, rising from somewhere deep in his stomach. Petko broke into voiceless sobbing. With his mouth open he coughed out a cry of grievance, gasping for breath in between fits of tears he could no longer hold. He cried only once when Lela died. He knew no tears, endured any pain.

When he finally got a hold of himself, he said softly:

"Please forgive me, Maria, for thinking so badly of you all these years. Thank you."

"Don't worry, brother. All these years I did not know myself who I was," Maria laughed off.

"That's not all," she continued, resuming her serious tone. *"You must be careful, say no word to no one! If Dana is indeed in some sort of*

trouble, and you do a silly thing to expose yourself to danger, there will be no one to help her. Here is what I say – you go to Brussels, do not go straight to their address, stay unnoticed, watch. If everything is OK, you just show up for a visit. If you see something suspicious, wait, watch, calculate and then act. Here is an address where you can stay. They are not Kalaidzhi, but they will take care of you. After all, we are all Gypsy."

Maria felt somewhat proud of herself for the first time in all those interminable years of scheming and calculating to survive in her brutal marriage. Now that she had finally gained respect or rather control over her frail husband, she felt needy of her true self. Only she did not quite remember any longer who her true self was, and there was no one to remind her. Sudden sadness confused her excitement. She wondered who she would have become if her father had chosen a different man for her husband.

"I must go now. I'll come in the morning. I'll bring hot soup for you and help you tidy up the place," she suggested, looking around in disapproval. *"What a mess! You should rest, Petko. Vitko will take you to the train station tomorrow morning."*

* * *

Petko could not wait for the morning. He went straight ahead to the city, hoping to catch the first available train.

His Jiguli broke halfway. He knew that it was high time his old car, his only friend throughout so many years, drew its last breath. He stroked it gently.

"So long, my friend, I have to leave you here."

A puff of smoke went off the engine as if bidding him good-bye. Petko turned away and walked toward the city lights. He did not look back.

The train station was closed when he finally reached it. He lay down on a bench and looked at the starry sky. He saw Lela. They were both lying in the field, watching the sky and kissing every time they spotted a shooting star. There, in the valley, Lela read to him, and later on to both him and Dana *The Arabian Nights* - an old book she had inherited from her mother.

"Where are you, Dana?!"

Slowly he sank into sleep. Lela was right next to him. He could now hear what she had whispered to him before.

"Lala, my redhead, my ruby!"

Petko did not take the morning train. His departure was not timed.

RUN,
NINON,
RUN

Tu lascerai ogne cosa
*diletta piú caramente**
Dante Allighieri, Paradise

Cold gusts of wind gasped spitefully among raging heaps of water, knitting them into a disorderly lace. The waves retreated in a soothing murmur of compromise and unequivocal acceptance of the wind's power. Polished by ages of compliance, the pebbles gave in with no resistance, allowing the waves to drag them along. Rain poured heavily from the starless, moonless sky. In the dismal darkness, her small figure stumbling along the coast was infinitesimal. She felt as if she was hurled into a primeval chaos and ceased to exist. The wild orchestra of the storm deafened her mind and disaccorded her body, which was refusing

---

* *You shall leave everything you love most.*

to obey her own will. Struggling to break free, to regain her "self", she pulled her weakened body against the wind. Eyes half closed, her face courageously took every single fierce slap of the wind. Her matted curls clasped her neck and fell clammy on her chest. Her feet slid over the pebbles, whose deceitful smoothness dragged her into the sea with every single step she fought through.

Hope kept her moving ahead. Flashes of lightning guided her way.

Interrupted by weeks of medically induced stupor, her escape had been thought out for months. She longed to be freed in a stormy darkness, to wake up to a morning of hope.

* * *

A man is sitting by an open window. He feels futile in his pursuit of words. Overwhelmed by his feelings, the verse escapes him. The search for words in self-exposure is tormenting. Where does he start and where does he end? The open notepad is full of crossed-out scribbles. He lifts his eyes to the sound of birds outside. The purple of the lilacs softly brushes the window frame. He takes a deep breath. He sees a sparrow pushing through the lilacs' blossoms.

"How prosaic," he thinks.

His mind takes off the verse he has been struggling to compose.

"Sparrows, grey and needy... always there..."

He looks away to slowly search the room. His gaze falls on a book of ancient Greek myths left open on the floor.

"The evil of Pandora's box...hope...hope could not fly out..." He takes a pen and quickly writes:

"hope comes and goes
it flickers, quivers, shudders

it flutters up
it crashes down
then suddenly strikes back"
He drops the pen.

"Hope is torture," he whispers closing his eyes.

He listens to his heart thumping rhythmically just like the clock on his desk, ticking time away.

"Hope must be free of reason," he thinks. *"Hope is free, even though Pandora trapped it in. There it stayed at the bottom of the box after evil spewed out to take over the world. Where is that bottom? Hope is not free. Was Nietzsche right? Is hope the worst of evils? Treacherously, it prolongs our torments."*

He hears his baby crying.

* * *

It was her fourth day on the run from the clinic. No food. No medication. Hunger made her stumble and fall now and then. But she staggered to her feet with her mind fresh and clear. The old hazy dreams and repetitive nightmares were fading away reluctantly. The dark shadows of unknown men were still all around, watching her, but they did not touch her. She felt almost at ease with their presence, taking them more as silent companions in her stormy escape.

* * *

A man tenderly rocks his baby girl to sleep. He sings a soft tune of love with no rhyme.

"Rhyme is too orderly, pretentious," he thinks. *"Rhyme is an effort of thought. It takes away the spontaneity of feeling..."*

He feels weak, exhausted. His soft murmuring of love lulls the baby to sleep. He holds her in his arms for yet a little longer, admiring her smiling grimace. Thoughts leave him. He is free of words. He kisses her tiny fingers, each one of them, and puts her gently into the cradle.

Twilight seeps into the room through an open window hushing the rowdy sparrows.

"Sparrows... so common... wither any weather, grey and unobtrusively present...how easily they fly in a straight path just with a blur of little wings..."

He wants to lie down and lose his thoughts again. In just a moment the dark will bring the quiet he has been longing for.

* * *

A young woman wept over the lifeless body of a man. She kept kissing his hand, which still felt warm and tender like it had always been when he made love to her. She curled herself up next to him on the floor in the purple puddle of blood. She pleaded him to wake up. Only he did not. The silver quiet of the full moon mercilessly poured in through the open window.

* * *

A baby girl wakes up to the sirens of police and ambulances. She does not cry. An unknown feeling of fear takes her breath away but not for long. She slowly pulls herself to sit up for the first time with no support and listens to the darkness of the room. She looks around for the familiar presence of a parent. She has already learned to love them both.

She is distracted and instantly amused by the moonlight, pouring in through the window. She tries to catch it with her tiny hands, but it slips away. She laughs at the moon's playfulness. The baby's joyful chuckles overpower the misery that has unfolded elsewhere in the house. The moonlight settles on her teddy bear. She falls back, trying to reach it, but sleep takes over, and she smiles.

"O what are you dreaming of, Ninon?!"

* * *

Ninon was five when her mother took her to a new big house. A man opened the door. He kissed her mother on the mouth and, holding her by the waist, led her inside. Nina signaled the little girl to follow. Ninon obeyed, hugging her teddy bear tightly. The man invited her to climb an unusually high staircase to her new room up in the attic. The old wood of the dark stairs gave a loud cracking sound now and then. It frightened the little girl. A feeling of fear took her breath away in a strange but familiar way. She stopped to listen and look around. She had felt that way before, but could not recall when, where, and why. She went on climbing the stairs, pushed by Yuri's hurrying hand.

* * *

"Do you like these sandals, Ninon?"

Yuri enjoyed buying new clothes for Ninon lately. Yuri's favorite stores were the huge cheap supermarkets with unsupervised cabins. The economic crisis had reduced both the number of customers and shop assistants. Curtained in the farthest corner, he would force Ninon into lengthy "*now-try-this-one-on*" sessions. The extra small adult size did not fit Ninon, leaving ample emptiness around her developing chest. He would unceremoniously watch the girl, blushing with embarrassment, undress. He would insist pulling a thing on and off, slewing his wet trembling hands all over her.

"These sandals are perfect. Keep them on," Yuri concluded, pulling Ninon's skirt up way too much and slithering his sticky fingers over her leg.

Trapped, scared and ashamed, Ninon felt.

He ordered her to put on a long stretch dress. He fixed a measuring look on her back. Her heart thumped with fear. She held her breath under Yuri's silent stare. Trembling, she folded her arms around her shoulders, covering her chest where Yuri now kept his eyes.

"We'll get it when your breasts are bigger," he finally said. *"Take it off."*

Ninon struggled to free herself from the long tube of polyester that clasped her head, shoulders, and arms. The more she pulled it, the more tightly it sucked in her face, leaving her breathless. Throbbing flesh suddenly pierced her, shooting arrows of pain into her stomach. He pushed and pushed, pressing her onto the cold mirror. He squeezed her breasts with one hand and her mouth with another. With her arms up, she was arrested in the endless suffocation of pain, Yuri, and polyester. Finally, he stopped and pulled the dress off.

Dizziness pulled her down. He grabbed her shoulders, roughly turned her to face his rotted breath, squeezed her cheeks painfully to unclench her teeth and forced his tongue down her throat. She choked with pain, fear, and disgust. He finally let go of her. She vomited. He zipped his pants up and ordered her to get dressed, wiping her off with that same dress she had been trapped in. She heard someone passing by the cabin. She wanted to call for help, but her voice failed her. Tears streamed down her face and neck.

"Don't you dare!" ordered Yuri with a murderously stern look. He grabbed some clothes and pulled her out of the cabin.

On the way to the cashier, Ninon felt that every single shelf Yuri pulled her by was mocking her. She could not hold her tears even against his shushing threats. He dragged her along, painfully squeezing her hand. Voiceless sobs broke out when they finally reached the cashier. A young woman with unkempt orange hair lazily greeted them and asked if everything was all right. She loudly smacked her huge red lips, chewing gum. Yuri responded that the girl was upset to not get everything she wanted. He casually flirted with the cashier while she scanned the items. With a nod of understanding the woman let the chewing gum pop out into a huge bubble and burst it on her red lips. The red mouth laughed saucily at Yuri's pleasantries.

Ninon stood by, violated and silent. She could not take her eyes off the smacking red lips that grew bigger and bigger and made her feel nauseated. Trying to hide her tears, she bent her head down. She saw her feet wearing the new sandals, which slowly blurred into Yuri's grin. His tongue slithered where the thin string threaded between her toes. A thin line of blood trickled down her legs. She fainted.

* * *

Ninon opened her eyes to the persistent sound of a motor. She was in the back seat of a car. Confused, she lifted her head and saw Yuri driving. He seemed preoccupied and did not notice that she was looking at him. She quietly slid down to hide behind his seat and closed her eyes. She did not recall how she got into the car, but the memory of what had happened in the supermarket rolled over her with a cold shiver.

She felt as if there was someone else sitting next to her. She half-opened her eyes and saw a girl, who looked exactly like her. The girl took her hand with both of hers and gently patted it. Ninon burst into tears. The girl slowly raised her hand to wipe off the tears streaming down Ninon's cold cheeks. Her hand felt soft and warm. Yuri looked back and said something to the girl. The girl ignored him.

When the car drove into the garage, the girl opened the door and left. Ninon watched her take the front seat in Nina's car. Nina ruffled the girl's hair just like she would do to Ninon's. Yuri waved at Nina as she drove away, Ninon waved too.

The girl did not come back. Ninon feared that Yuri had dealt with her just like he threatened to get rid of Nina.

* * *

Ninon's mother said that God had too many grievances to take care of. Ninon silently hoped that He would notice her too. Nina could not stop scolding her for her bizarre change from a playful little girl into a "gloomy stranger". She kept preaching Ninon on the suffering of millions of people victimized in genocide or dying from famine. Ninon had to be thankful, her mother said. She had to be grateful for a stepfather like Yuri, who was the reason for their immense comfort.

At school Ninon was not favored by her teachers, nor did she have any friends. Her voice was too small and her work was never good enough. She spent hours staring at open textbooks filled with long lines of words. But those words had no sense to hold on to or to remember. Parents were called to the school, teachers were frustrated, her mother was out too often, and Yuri was always in. She sought to avoid him. But the staircase was a trap.

* * *

Twilight seeps in through an open window.

"Twilight...the border between dark and light," Alex once wrote.

Ninon opens a drawer and takes out a paper. The paper is old and torn unevenly on one side. She has found it wrapped around a smooth purple crystal in a box with her mother's old belongings. The crystal slipped away into a crack between the floorboards. Ninon could not get it out, but she has kept the paper. It is a poem full of crossed-out words. She reads it whispering like a prayer:

"the pink gold of sunset fades to a hundred hues of grey
light hurries its escape to disavow the wasteful day
into the dark it flees like a chameleon
or am I simply lost in an oblivion?
like any other living soul
worth of nothing all along?"

" the dark devours greedily its daily prey of light
the light that struggles through the hills
and tops of trees
and drowning
in the seas"

"tell me
light rests behind that mountain
to find new strength and to return
to yet the same horizon?"

"the light regains
the strength of bliss
to pick the fallen from the abyss
or rather merciless
it shines deceitfully
to blind

to render sightless
the one who stumbles, falls and sees no more"

"bliss is ignorance"

"tell me
is there a horizon with no light?"

"the silence of twilight
perturbs the wretchedness of mind
the wretchedness of mine"

Ninon takes her eyes off the paper. She listens to the birds. Sparrows, so many by her window, are they the keepers of her shameful secret? Grey and ever-present, their simplicity is inviting.

"Sparrows are the ugliest of birds," Yuri would say.

Ninon grabs a handful of her unruly red curls, the object of Yuri's admiration, and snips them off with scissors. Her feet angrily stomp over the cut curls. She will be grey like sparrows. She looks out of the window, but the birds are neither seen nor heard. The sun has left. The nature has bowed in a silent respect to acknowledge its departure.

The silence of twilight is deafening yet intriguing. With her eyes closed, she longs for a new day before the present one is gone.

* * *

Nina's drinking drove her out to parties almost daily. Left alone, Ninon listened to the sounds of the house. She often thought of her father lately. Although rather than a thought, it was more of a feeling of emptiness that only loneliness could evoke, the feeling of longing for something that was lost forever, yet never had been known. Sometimes she felt as if he was somewhere beside her, close but helpless in his wordlessness.

* * *

The staircase. A wordless, voiceless image of torture persecuted her. She knew the different cracking sounds of every single step leading up to her room in the attic. He was on step three. Ten more left. The steps moaned loudly under Yuri's imposing weight. 5... 8... 10... louder... louder... deafening... She threw the door open to run down and away.

* * *

A woman found her daughter on the stairs in the arms of her husband. Painfully yanking her hair, the woman pulled the girl's face close to hers. The woman reeked of perfume, alcohol and cigarettes. She gave the girl's face a fierce slap. Some loud talking with Yuri followed. He promptly led her away to the bedroom and shut the door.

The woman quickly came to terms with her husband. Indeed, he was the victim of a vicious attack by her hateful daughter. He assured her that the abhorrent incident was the first of its kind.

"Look, Nina," he spoke convincingly, having masterly loaded his tone with the right amount of hearty concern, *"the girl was late from school, she most probably smokes pot, they all do, so she's lost her senses! Look what she has done to her hair!"*

Ninon shook in disgust at Yuri's accusations, but words failed her again. Defenseless, she stood there in her speechlessness.

"Boarding school! Run by nuns!" the woman shrieked with a voice hoarse from alcohol and misery.

* * *

Ninon knows God has heard her prayers. O that thought of leaving the house of plenty! A smile won't leave her face. She examines her face in the mirror. She likes her new reflection.

Ninon falls asleep with happy thoughts. She dreams of being free in a faraway place. She dreams of reading her father's poems from that secret notebook that Nina promised to give her when she grows up. She dreams of words finding their way to her thoughts, of friends finding their way to her life, of her mother finding a way to love her again. The smile keeps her dreams safe.

* * *

Sun rays beam through the curtains. Ninon rolls to the sunniest spot on her pillow and lets the sun caress the freckles on her nose, just like in the old days when she used to wake up in her mother's arms.

Their small studio on the outskirts of the city could fit only a few things with most of the room taken up by an old sofa. Nina used to hold her little girl tightly in her sleep as if afraid to lose her. After Alex was gone, everything was gone one by one – friends, house, hope. Little Ninon was the only thing she could hold onto to harbor her loneliness.

* * *

"Loneliness is a painful illness of the soul," Alex once wrote. *"The chemistry of its pain is immeasurable. There is neither medicine to treat it, nor precaution to take. Slowly, it penetrates one's soul and metastases into the body, draining it of vitality. In different doses, loneliness is indispensable to everyone's life, just like happiness, love, hatred... There are many ways to acquire loneliness to a different extent of misery that unfolds as a consequence. Whether it depends on us or not,*

we decry loneliness as a will of merciless destiny. Is destiny the causal excuse for a wounded commitment?"

* * *

A flashlight runs through a thick curtain of rain and fixes on Ninon's face, blinding her. Her mouth is parched with thirst. Her will to stay focused gets drowned in a painful spasm of hunger. She does not know where the endless shoreline has brought her. An old woman's face is leaning over hers. The woman's hand wipes water off her face just like that girl once wiped off her tears, with the warmth of compassion. The woman's soft voice lulls her to sleep. A smile will keep her safe.

* * *

A newborn baby girl is a delight the man could not have expected. He cradles her in his arms. His lullaby is a song of love with no rhyme. He will be leaving soon.

"Ninon, your smile is beautiful," he whispers to the sleeping baby.

* * *

Although his half-Russian father always claimed that he had named his son after the greatest Russian poet Alexander Pushkin, Alex's mother was convinced that her husband, an ardent admirer of dystopia, had the main protagonist of *A Clockwork Orange* deep in mind. Alex also thought so lately. He had always felt as an alternate to hope as if doomed to embrace the mass of societal misery and negativity brought upon him by his father's choice. As a teenager, he had been often requested to sit through the lengthy philosophical discussions of his father's friends. Cautious not to disappoint his father, Alex never refused. Too young to follow their opinionated arguments, he would tap his foot softly, playing words in *terza rima,* which he had learned to admire Dante for. It was during one of such evenings that Alex had attempted his first venture into poetry. Later on, he understood that his "*flair for writing*" was less of a talent and more of an imposition bestowed upon him by his father. His ambitious literary father read *The Canterbury Tales* as bedtime stories to little Alex, burdening him with a perturbed sleep. Later on, the vernacular language popularized by Chaucer, had overpowered Alex to such an extent that words simply failed him.

* * *

Alex looks at the blossoms of lilacs pushing through the window. In the fading daylight, they are deep purple, throwing shade on the open book of ancient Greek myths.

"*Damn you, Dionysus,*" he whispers, "*your beasts have chased my pure maiden. She is a stone, an empty crystal.*"

His thought flows from Nina's drinking to an amethyst crystal left long forgotten in his desk drawer. His mother used to put this small polished stone under his pillow for safe dreams. He remembers her as a beautiful young woman from his faraway childhood in a faraway home, cheerfully serving his favorite pasta and singing in her native Italian. He looks at the crystal, searching his memory for the feeling of fascination he once had for its purple depth. Now, many years later the stone is the only memory of the country he left so long ago.

"*You've been lost in my drawers just like my roots got lost in this country,*" Alex whispers, twisting the stone in his fingers.

He walks back to Ninon's room and puts the crystal under her pillow. He takes the baby's hand and kisses her tiny fingers, each one of them.

He wants to lie down and lose his thoughts again.

* * *

A man is leaving. Unlike his past business and leisure trips, this time, his departure is not scheduled, he has neither train, nor plane, nor bus to catch. Time does not oblige him any longer. His will is his carrier. His destination is unknown. A letter might be expected. But words have no feelings just like his feelings have neither meanings nor rhymes.

"Ninon, I'll leave at twilight. I'll live the day and will be gone before the night falls. Your smile will keep you safe."

* * *

The walls in the ward were a glazed white with occasional specks of red – the reminders of other inhabitants' will to protect themselves from blood-sucking mosquitos. The door was locked at all times, except when a nurse brought in meals and medication. Ninon could use a red button to call a nurse, only no one would come.

The window had no curtains. At night, Ninon saw men on the other side of the window. They stood on a staircase and stared at her with a particular smirk, like Yuri's. She hid her head under the blanket. Medication plunged her into a sleepless drowse, but the smirk and the staircase stayed, tenaciously clinging to her mind.

Day broke in. Ninon felt exhausted. She stayed alert through her sleep, hiding from the men who came out of the wall and whispered like Yuri did - right into her ear.

A doctor appeared at the door and a number of white gowns poured into the room. Ninon could not take her eyes off the wall and Yuri's slithering tongue sticking out of it. The white gowns were saying something, but words had long lost their meaning for her.

The gowns left. The wall softened its glare. Yuri vanished. She looked out of the window. The staircase disappeared giving way to bougainvillea bushes. An old man sat on a bench, talking to himself. The sun hit back inside. She closed her eyes and surrendered to the medication and the same nightmare – Yuri, the staircase, her ears deafened by his laughter, the loud moaning of the old wooden steps, her body flailing helplessly in pain, squirming at the need to vomit.

* * *

The sunrays gently caress her freckles. She is awake, going over a happy thought of a boarding school. No one calls her for breakfast. She hears Nina speaking over the phone in a hushed tone. She will not go to school today. She will be packed and gone soon. She hears her mother coming up the stairs. Nina's light walking makes the steps murmur in a delightful confusion. Ninon's heart is beating fast. Her face is blushing. She wants to look into Nina's eyes. She longs for Nina to hug her tightly, just like she used to do when they lived, the two of them, in their small studio on the shabby but joyful outskirts of the city.

Nina's entrance feels awkward. Her gracefulness is gone. She looks suddenly aged. The usual blue of her eyes is sulkily grey. She does not look into her daughter's eyes.

* * *

"No boarding school," Yuri reconsidered.

When the sober Nina announced her decision to pressure Ninon to confess if she had taken drugs, Yuri panicked he might be exposed. He took Nina's hand and, kissing it with the right amount of gentleness, said that he had meant to talk to her about Ninon's bizarre behavior. He told Nina how he watched the girl do strange things for weeks and weeks.

"Why didn't you tell me before?!"

"Darling, when could I?! You are never home!"

Yuri kept on complaining how deeply he was hurt by the incident. He slipped on the stairs and the girl jumped on him and pulled him on top of her with an evidently failed intention to seduce him, and he struggled to let go of her! That was exactly what Nina saw upon her unexpected arrival.

"Ninon must go into therapy," Yuri concluded, *"her father killed himself. She might be a psychiatric case too!"*

"Alex was not sick," Nina said coldly.

Yuri ignored her comment and continued with more "evidence" proving that Ninon was undeniably delirious. As perfect a stepfather as he was, he had already arranged for a psychiatrist.

* * *

Ninon loved Nina dearly. Her mother meant everything to her, she admired her every word, her every single gesture. But Nina became so unreachable lately, always out, back in late. She barely noticed Ninon.

"Nina will be gone and never found if you dare to disclose that we love each other," Yuri threatened Ninon after that fitting session when he murdered both her childhood and that other girl - the unknown, yet the closest friend she had ever had. Enslaved by the fear and abuse, Ninon succumbed to suffering in silence.

* * *

The white gowns spoke more distinctly now. They asked her questions to which she had no answers. She looked into their faces, but her gaze was lost. The ward was no longer locked.

The doctor asked again and again why she had tried to kill herself. She was confused. All she remembered was her longing for life, the life where the sun played with her freckles and her mother laughed, holding her in her arms.

* * *

Another session. She can no longer focus on the doctor's words. She hears a soft man's voice coming from somewhere behind the doctor's chair. It sounds so painstakingly familiar, its warmth brings tears to her eyes. She gets up and slowly walks towards the voice. She stretches her arms out, but cannot reach the shadow behind the doctor's chair.

A male nurse rushes to the doctor's alarm. He twists Ninon's arms and carries her out of the doctor's office.

* * *

Ninon did not remember how long she had stayed at the hospital. Now that the medication's dose was lowered, she noticed that her curls had grown back.

"It must have been awhile," she thought, examining her changed face in the mirror.

Who she saw looking back at her was not her, the Ninon she had known before. It was Nina, her mother. Nina looked straight into her eyes now.

"I love you," she said sadly. Tears streamed down her face.

A huge blue bubble splashed onto Nina's face.

"Oops, sorry," an old woman said, brushing her toothless mouth at the sink next to Ninon.

With a wide-open mouth, she spat toothpaste all around.

"Tears, ah?" the woman asked, staring at Ninon with a toothless smile.

Ninon slowly walked back to the ward.

Another woman sat on a bed, staring at her swinging feet and singing *Jingle Bells*. The woman tried to make her feet catch up with the tune, but they refused to oblige. Ninon stayed at the doorway, startled by the scene and unwilling to disturb the woman's effort. The woman slowly lifted her head and gave Ninon an empty look. Her mouth disfigured in an attempted smile.

This disfigured smile struck Ninon as an appalling reflection of her own disfigured life. Confined to a hospital and heavy medication by Yuri's malicious scheme, she realized that she had no hope of being free anytime soon, perhaps never at all.

The voice she had heard at the doctor's office reappeared.

"Run, Ninon, run!"

"God is the father," the priest often told Ninon.

Ninon knew now that it was her long-lost wordless father who was speaking to her.

* * *

"... she will take off in a storm to wash away her voiceless sorrows."

UN®EGISTERED

"My life is my message"
Mahatma Gandhi

A group of soldiers ceremoniously mounted a flag on top of Ayanganna Mountain. On its way up the flag slackened, clinging to the pole, then straightened out, revealing its golden arrow. The arrow darted out as if ready to fly, but the wind restrained it and launched it in the opposite direction. In just a few hours Guyana would immerse into Mashramani festivities, celebrating its independence. The brightly masqueraded nation would pour into the carnival-arrayed streets of the capital. Music, amplified by Banks beer and Demerara rum, would weave the colorful crowds of dancing women and men into a rhythmically swaying stream.

* * *

With an expression of stupor in her large black eyes, Taniasha listened to the sound of drums, wafting from afar. Her absent gaze was fixed on the baby she had just given birth to.

In the dim light of an early morning hour, the baby looked to her like an old dark ball that her brother, Roy, had kicked about. A mass of black hair spiked up from the baby's head. A strange sound came out of its mouth that was so big it seemed to have taken up almost all of its face.

"Who is this baby?" Taniasha thought all of a sudden.

The drums got louder, more instruments fused into the festive rhythm. Music and singing filled the air with the first sun rays, breaking through the window of the delivery ward.

"The carnival is on its way," said the nurse, swaddling the baby. *"You are born on a special day, little Mash!"*

The nurse turned to Taniasha and said something, but her words got drowned out by the carnival laughter, bursting in from outside. Chanting and drumming bounced heavily between Taniasha's temples. She closed her eyes.

* * *

Thin branches crackled in the fire, intruding upon the dusk orchestra of cicadas in the rainforest jungle. A young boy and an old woman sat by the fire, slowly chewing on their cassava supper.

"Rivers do not come from nowhere," the old woman said to the boy. *"Potaro, the river of our people, comes from Ayanganna Mesa. Gods used to stop there to rest on top of it. Tomorrow is the day when our land became free. Mashramani! Soldiers will raise our flag on Ayanganna Mesa and we'll celebrate our freedom, Roy. Rivers do not end nowhere, Roy,"* she continued solemnly.

"Potaro, the river of our people, flows into Essequibo – the river that is even bigger! Without our river, the other river, that carries our

water far away from our land, will not be strong. This is how life is, Roy. We do not end nowhere."

* * *

The morning had long declared its sunny presence.

Nurse Marjory sat in silence by Taniasha's bed, holding the girl's small hand and thinking that she was lucky to have survived. A week earlier, she helped take this twelve-year-old girl off the helicopter that brought her, unconscious, to Georgetown hospital from Mahdia. In the early hours of Mashramani, Taniasha gave birth to a baby girl, whom everyone now called Mash.

Taniasha had not spoken a word in days. Every morning nurse Marjory came to talk. But looking at Taniasha's absent face, she wondered if she should give up the effort.

* * *

The old woman moved closer to the fire. She unfolded a thin blanket and covered the boy, who curled up by the fire, shivering with fever. She put a wet cloth on his forehead. The boy gave her a grateful look of relief. He did not speak but continued looking at her intently as if asking for something else.

"Many years ago," the old woman started, *"a murderous disease took over our nation, the nation of Patamona."*

The boy smiled faintly, content that his wordless request for a story was understood.

"Many families died, leaving no one behind," the old woman continued slowly.

The boy's face saddened.

"The Spirits! The Spirits were upset with the Patamonas! Many sacrifices had been brought in countless attempts to please the Spirits.

But the disease kept sweeping the Patamonas away. Nor did it spare the legendary Kaie, the wisest chief of the Patamonas. Kaie, the mighty warrior, who had won the battles with the Caribs, was the strongest of our people. The disease brought an unbearable suffering upon him, but he had never complained. He was as silent in pain as you are, my boy."

The old woman gently caressed the boy's head and continued: *"Seeing the disease spreading so fast that only a few Patamonas were left alive, Kaie called the wisest men for a meeting. They chanted for several days, calling for the Spirits to unveil the reason for their anger. Finally, the oldest shaman revealed that Makonaima, the Great Spirit, wanted a sacrifice to be offered to him at the spot where the river fell the deepest. Without hesitation, Kaie announced that he would be the sacrifice. That night our nation gathered around Kaie, in tears. It was not easy for them to imagine life without their greatest leader. That night was just like ours now, peaceful and sad."*

The old woman went silent. Her eyes, dark as night, fixed on the fire. Tears softened their harsh empty darkness, filling it with the burning sadness of the blazing firelight. She lived alone for many years with no one to speak to but herself. Often, she was not aware when her speaking faded away and her thoughts took over. The boy gently pulled on her sleeve. Reminded of his presence, the woman continued:

"Painted for festivities, our people sadly moved to the place where Potaro cut off its peaceful flow and fell deeply in one wholesome thunderous drop. There, ahead of us," the woman pointed at the darkness, *"a big fire was started. The best food was brought and shared. The fire burned throughout the night. The dance of sacrifice was performed with sadness. When dawn broke in, the fire was put to ashes. Kaie asked his people to leave him alone with his daughters. Slowly, people moved away, respectfully keeping their distance in waiting. Kaie's daughters kissed his hand and helped him into a canoe, which was adorned with the most precious treasures. Kaie sat there, somber in*

silence...the silence that was about to take him in forever. He had never felt so willing to let himself go into the eternal peace of non-existence. The river gently accepted the gift-laden sacrifice, slowly floating the beautiful canoe downstream... from where we are now."

The boy peered into the dark, and for a second he felt as if the Great Kaie, grand and somber, was out there in his canoe, floating away into the grey mist of dawn. Goosebumps crept over him. He curled up tightly.

"When the canoe reached the end of the river," continued the old woman, *"water seized hold of it in a majestic thunderous swirl. The Great Spirit picked Kaie up and carried him away. At that very moment, the sun came out, birds burst into song, and animals woke up in the forest. The people of the Patamona nation knew that Makonaima, the Great Spirit, had been appeased. This very place, where the Great Spirit had taken away our Kaie, the Kaieteur Falls, is now right out there, next to us, my little Roy. At dawn, we'll celebrate our Mashramani!"*

The old woman went silent again. The boy pulled on her sleeve again, but she did not respond. She told him the story of Kaie many times, but it was the first time that she had told it differently. The one she had told before said that the Great Kaie sacrificed himself to save the Patamonas from unending wars with the Caribs. At school, though, the story of Kaieteur Falls told that a grumpy old man was brought to the waterfall and shoved off by his family. From that time on, the waterfall was called "an-old-man-fall" or Kaieteur Falls. Confused, the boy kept staring at the old woman, but she had grown too distant in her silence.

"Sleep Roy. We must be up early," she finally responded.

* * *

Ralph's camp was deep in the forest. Gold mining was the occupation he had chosen as a young Amerindian. The jungle was full of illegal miners, but Ralph was native to the Kaieteur area and had no legal constraints to practicing this profession. There was no one in his tribe, who could teach him the trade, so he had to work as an apprentice for an illegal miner. Raised in the jungle, he knew every little deviation the river had made over the years. His instinct had never failed him in finding a generous gold vein or "mother lode", although he had to take his employer deeper and deeper into the forest ravaged by pork-knockers.

Surviving for months on pickled pork, miners, known for that reason as "pork-knockers", kept destroying the jungle and polluting its rivers with mercury. They cut trees by every single water source. They washed the gold out and left pools of stagnant water, breeding mosquitoes and feeding mercury into the soil and rivers.

Having decided to prosper from the abundance of the wealth hidden in the soil of his land, Ralph soon understood why the children in his village were born with defects, and why the men and women kept losing their memory and physical abilities. Malaria, dengue fever, and typhoid were nothing next to the insidious mercury poisoning that was taking his people away. Persecuted by the thought of the destruction that the thirst for wealth had brought upon his land, Ralph felt enslaved in his own emotional torment. He searched for ways to get out of his commitments, but he had no other means to provide for his wife and their newborn child.

Just like any other small camp, Ralph's camp was set in an opening by a water source. A tent mounted at the edge of the opening with pipes and shovels scattered around.

Despite an easier life at Ralph's service, the site of the camp disgusted Taniasha with its muddy dirtiness and the memories of hard labor and abuse, the memories that she was so eager yet unable to erase.

* * *

A man knocked on the door of Oley's hut.

Oley's wife, Radika, had put this hut together out of old wood planks years ago. She used to sell pots in Mahdia, a small provincial town nearby. One day she came back with a pile of used wood on top of an old truck. She gave Oley a bottle of rum and ordered the driver to help her. The driver took to work without looking at Oley. Sipping on his rum, Oley silently watched the driver's hand go under his wife's skirt every time she went up the ladder. But with a bottle of rum, Oley did not bother.

Oley did not remember how many years had passed since malaria had taken Radika away. The hut was now falling apart, washed out by heavy rains. But a bottle of rum put everything in place almost daily. Some mornings, when he was soberer, he would ask himself if the children his wife had left him with were indeed his, but the doubts easily abandoned him over a bottle.

Having knocked for a while with no answer, the man pulled the door open. He knew Oley was there, always lying drunk on his old bamboo mat.

"Where is your daughter?" he asked.

Oley did not remember where Taniasha was lately. The last time he saw her was weeks ago when he sold her to an old porkknocker.

"We agreed that you'd send her with me for the new season," the man insisted.

"Take Roy instead," Oley mumbled.

The man hesitated, then asked, "How much?"

"Three bottles per day," Oley thrust his three fingers almost into the man's face.

"I'll give you one," said the man firmly and walked out. He left a few bottles of rum on the floor. Oley made an attempt to count them, but, drunk as he already was, he could not pass beyond three. He gave up counting and opened a bottle.

He was on his second bottle when the man came back saying that the *"little bastard"* was nowhere to be found. The man demanded his bottles back. Squeezing a joint between his black-and-yellow rotting teeth, Oley stretched out on the floor and roared with laughter. Thick saliva gathered at the corners of his dry cracked lips. Shaking with insane laughter, he waved the man to leave.

* * *

"Wake up, Roy," said the old woman.

The boy was not asleep. With his eyes closed, he listened to the silent forest. The chilly morning made him shiver under the blanket in which he had muffled himself. He opened his eyes to the old woman's voice. She sat at the same spot as before he had fallen asleep. She had kept the fire burning through the night, but it was now dying out. A light breeze picked up the ashes and threw them playfully into the boy's face. He giggled, hiding under the blanket. The old woman smiled sadly, thinking of her own childhood, the husband she had loved, the daughters she had lost. She brought her grandson to Kaieteur Falls to pay obeisance to the Great Spirit and to plead with Him for a mercy over her family, of which only Roy and Taniasha had remained.

* * *

They slowly walked along the river. The morning mist, rising from the waterfall, left nothing to the eye, slithering up trees and thickly enveloping the jungle. After a few steps, the old woman stopped. She pulled the boy to the river and told him to step in. She held his arm in a strong grip.

"The holy water will wash your pain away, Roy," she said calmly.

The boy shivered with cold but obeyed. The confidence with which she spoke, and the strength with which she held his arm, made him trust her.

* * *

Taniasha's stomach felt bloated. Her bosom swelled, and vomiting tortured her in the mornings. She felt as if she would die soon, just like her mother did. She was not sure whether she should be saddened or happy to leave the life she did not own. Nonetheless, she kept putting cassareep* on her belly and chest, hoping that the healing liquid, used so often by her late mother, would help her feel better. But her stomach kept growing bigger and bigger, and she felt as if something was in there that was not hers, perhaps an evil spirit. At school, she was told to see a Cuban doctor, who worked in Mahdia. Earlier, a friend of hers had also grown a stomach, and the doctor took her away in his car. Taniasha was sure that her disease was different from malaria that killed her mother. But she feared that she might have become infectious like Roy.

She often thought of her little brother, hoping that he was recovering from his illness far away from their sad motherless home.

"It would be nice to leave," she thought.

The thought of leaving visited her often. She knew some girls who left for the city. The woman, who came every year to recruit young girls to serve seasonal workers in the city, offered Taniasha a good salary. But she had to take care of Roy and her ailing father. If she had gone away, her little brother would have had to take over her work. Her father sent her to do service to pork-knockers right after her mother died. She was seven when he sold her to her first client. He got rum in return and a small amount of money.

---

* *A liquid made from cassava root and used by Amerindians as both a spice for cooking and an antiseptic ointment.*

The meals that their money could afford were poor and consisted mostly of cassava, grown by Taniasha, and Coca-Cola.

Once at work, Taniasha had to miss school. Sometimes she cleaned for the miners, but they mostly hired her for their nightly needs. She learned to undress quickly in order to avoid the heavy hand of drunken men, striking the back of her head.

She ran away once but had to go back because when she had reached home, she saw Roy being taken in her place. She ran after the Jeep that carried Roy away to the camp, but she was too late to catch up with it. She walked back to the pork-knockers' camp, and when she had reached it that night, she heard Roy crying in the tent from which she had escaped. Through the tent's opening, she watched the two miners passing her little brother from one to another. Roy begged them to stop, but their drunken laughter was the only response he got. Later, they threw him out of the tent. When the light died out, Taniasha picked up her bleeding brother and carried him home. In the morning, when they had finally reached the village, her father shamed her for having forced her brother to work instead of her.

Roy got very ill since then. He never talked again, and did not go to school. Taniasha was afraid that he had caught malaria. She put cassareep to his head that was always hot with fever just like her mother's before she died. She sent several messages to her grandmother, whom she had never met, and who lived by the waterfalls of Potaro. But weeks went by before the old woman could arrive.

The old woman brought a nurse; they took Roy somewhere and brought him back soon, saying that he had AIDS. Taniasha had not heard of such a disease, but she was told that cassareep would not help.

When the old woman arrived, she cried and argued with Oley in the brief intervals of his sobriety. A few days later she left, taking Roy with her.

Oley sent Taniasha away to that same camp. Several weeks later, Taniasha's stomach got bloated.

* * *

Mahdia's clinic was freshly painted and had nets on its windows that opened to the yard. There were three donkeys and a motorcycle, parked by the entrance door.

Taniasha walked in, accompanied by her employer, Ralph. In fact, he was not her employer. An old pork-knocker, who hired her, got gravely sick with malaria and went away, leaving Ralph, his apprentice, to take care of the mine. At first, Ralph insisted that she go back to school, but she told him that if she came back to the village, her father would sell her to someone else immediately. Ralph let her stay around.

She liked the camp life for the first time. No drunken father, no pork-knockers. She had plenty of time to think. But should she?

She had never had many thoughts except for the ones of fear and escape. Her father's drunken anger and her brother's sad eyes did not allow even those two thoughts to evolve. At the school that she attended, interrupted by her frequent "employment", the teacher often spoke of "dreaming". Taniasha thought that she would have definitely failed that assignment if given as homework. Then she thought she was thinking too much, and that too much thinking was bad.

"Thinking is a disease," said her father when she brought Roy from the miner's camp after that dreadful night. *"Your thinking made your brother ill! Your thinking made me lose the good old clients!"* He accompanied his words with a strong slap, stamping her face with a bruise that stayed there for more than a week, reminding her of her terrible mistake.

Since Roy got ill, Taniasha was afraid of thinking.

Ralph lived without noticing her as if she was not around. But once he looked at her, surprised, and asked her of her growing belly. She broke into tears, fearing that he would send her away. Ralph did not send her away. Instead, he drove her in his old Jeep to see the Cuban doctor.

The doctor's office smelled of a freshness she had not known before. An old miner once gave Taniasha a small bottle of liquid that he called "perfume", and asked her to spray it on her neck for the night.

"Perhaps this is perfume," she thought, looking at the neatly arranged shelves and chairs.

She was asked to wait until Ralph had finished speaking to the doctor.

The doctor was a young handsome man. His face wore a kind smile and a pair of glasses in a large black frame. He invited Taniasha to undress behind the screen. She had taken off her clothes so many times at the demand of her clients, but she now felt deeply embarrassed with this handsome young man asking her to undress. A nurse came in and gave her a white sheet to cover herself. Taniasha felt even more embarrassed, blaming herself for thinking of a doctor inappropriately. She blushed with shame and confusion.

The doctor told her that there was a baby growing inside her.

* * *

The Cuban doctor knocked on Oley's door.

Oley did not get up to open.

Through the cracks between the wood planks, the doctor could see Oley lying on a floor mat, surrounded by empty bottles.

The doctor pulled the door. It yielded with a loud squeak. Oley did not move, neither did he breathe.

The lady, who accompanied the doctor and Taniasha to Oley's hut, said that Tanisha had no documents. Neither her birth nor the birth of her brother, Roy, was registered.

"They do not exist, just like many other Amerindian children," said the lady.

She took Taniasha's hand and led her away.

A few days later Taniasha woke up to nurse Marjory.

* * *

The old woman dried the boy with a fresh cloth that she had prepared and kept untouched throughout their long journey. His thin body was shivering with cold and fever. He held his breath to suppress his loud coughing. He was afraid to disturb the Great Spirit. But more than that, he felt embarrassed to make his weakness seen by the Great Kaie.

The old woman helped Roy put on his new clothes. She spent all her savings to get him the best pair of shoes and a suit with a white shirt. The suit hung loosely on him but it did not matter.

She asked the boy to turn away and wait until she washed too. She slowly dipped her wrinkly hands into the water. The weeds streamed softly through her trembling fingers, disfigured by hard work and arthritis. She stepped deeper into the river and let the weeds wash her. She took a water lily, nestled off the stream, and fixed it in her hair just like she used to do when she was young. She put on a colorful skirt and an embroidered blouse that she had prepared long ago for her burial.

The old woman took Roy's hand and looked into his eyes.

"Do not fear, my son," she said softly. *"Today is the day of Mashramani, the day of our freedom. Remember, Roy, we do not fall and we do not end nowhere."*

They both stepped into the water. Roy held his grandmother's hand tightly. This old woman whom he had known for only a few months was his only family now. She had stayed with him at the hospital. She had told him stories about plants and animals. She had told him the story of the Great Kaie. She had held him in her arms when he shivered with fever. Although he was only eight years old, he understood that he was a boy with no identity, an outcast with an incurable disease.

They walked the shallow waters slowly in silence. They both thought of Taniasha. Roy thought of the time when they had kicked around his old dark ball, the only toy he had had. The old woman thought of Taniasha's large black eyes filled with tears, the eyes that she could not look into when she was taking Roy away.

"Let the Great Spirit free you," she whispered.

The carpet of weeds felt soft under their feet as they kept stepping further in. They walked past the water lilies, sheltered beautifully in large families in the little pockets by the shore. They could feel the stream inviting them deeper in. The mist cleared, the sun rose, gliding its golden rays over the water. Their fear left them, and so did their thoughts. Their dreams were long lost too. As the river got deeper and the stream grew stronger, the woman took the boy into her arms. He hugged her tightly and closed his eyes.

And the river fell in a majestic thunderous drop, bearing its waters into Essequibo.